Barbie™ in Princess POWER

Adapted by Mary Tillworth
Based on the original screenplay by Marsha Griffin
Illustrated by Ulkutay Design Group

Special thanks to Venetia Davie, Ryan Ferguson, Sarah Lazar, Charnita Belcher, Tanya Mann, Julia Phelps, Nicole Corse, Sharon Woloszyk, Rita Lichtwardt, Carla Alford, Rob Hudnut, David Wiebe, Shelley Dvi-Vardhana, Gabrielle Miles, Julie Osborn, Rainmaker Entertainment, and Patricia Atchison and Zeke Norton

 A GOLDEN BOOK · NEW YORK

Published in the United States by Golden Books, an imprint of Random House Children's Books, a division of Random House LLC, 1745 Broadway, New York, NY 10019, and in Canada by Random House of Canada Limited, Toronto, Penguin Random House Companies. No part of this book may be reproduced or copied in any form without permission from the copyright owner. Golden Books, A Golden Book, A Little Golden Book, the G colophon, and the distinctive gold spine are registered trademarks of Random House LLC.
randomhousekids.com
Educators and librarians, for a variety of teaching tools, visit us at RHTeachersLibrarians.com
ISBN: 978-0-553-50741-6 (trade) — ISBN: 978-0-553-50742-3 (ebook)
Printed in the United States of America
10 9 8 7 6 5 4 3 2 1

On a lovely day in the faraway kingdom of Windemere, Princess Kara was in trouble—again! Her best friends, Madison and Makalya, had built her a flying machine, and Kara had crashed it into a tree!

"You could have been injured—or worse!" the queen cried as Kara climbed down.

"The world is more dangerous than you realize," added the king.

Kara longed to be brave and daring, but her parents wanted to protect her from every danger.

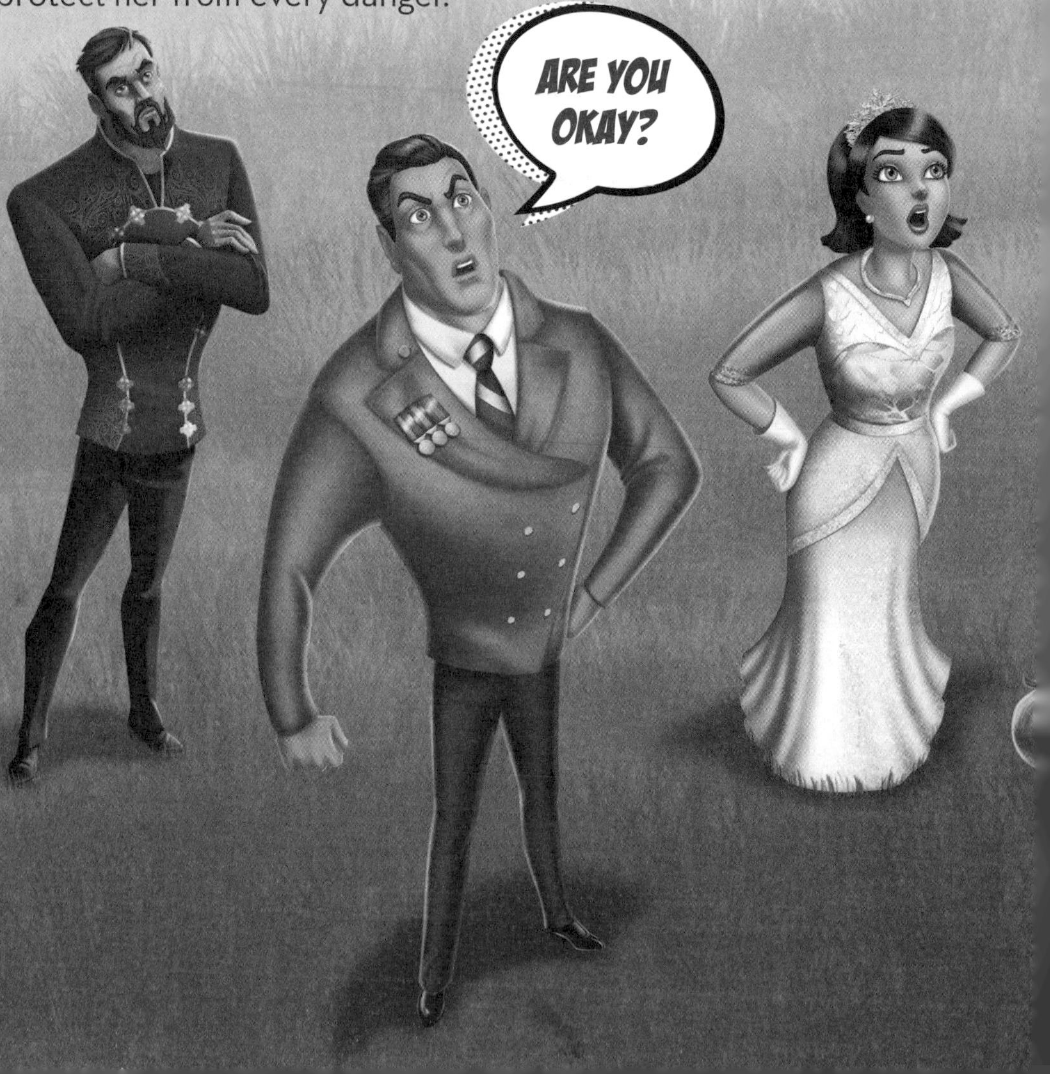
ARE YOU OKAY?

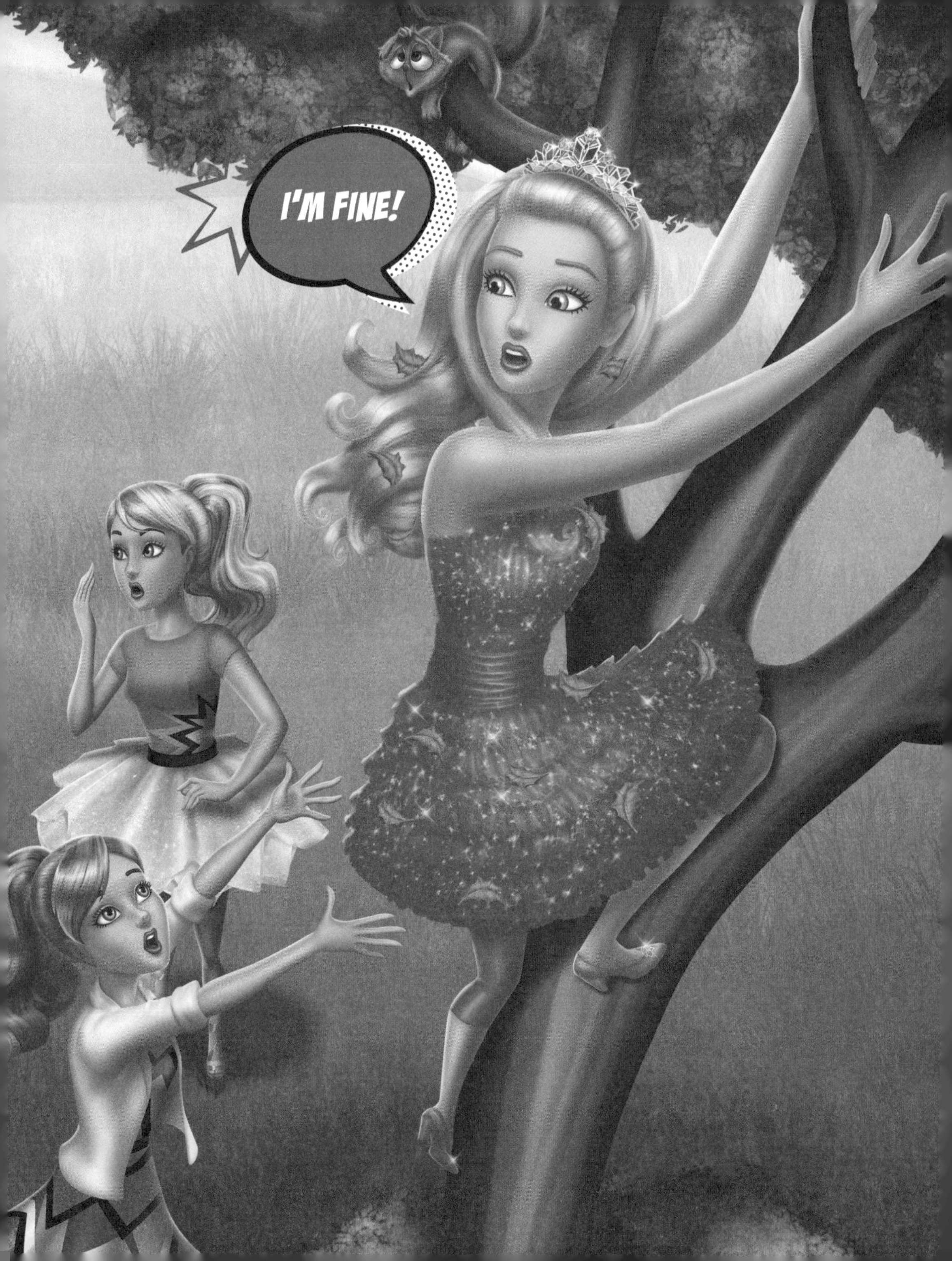
I'M FINE!

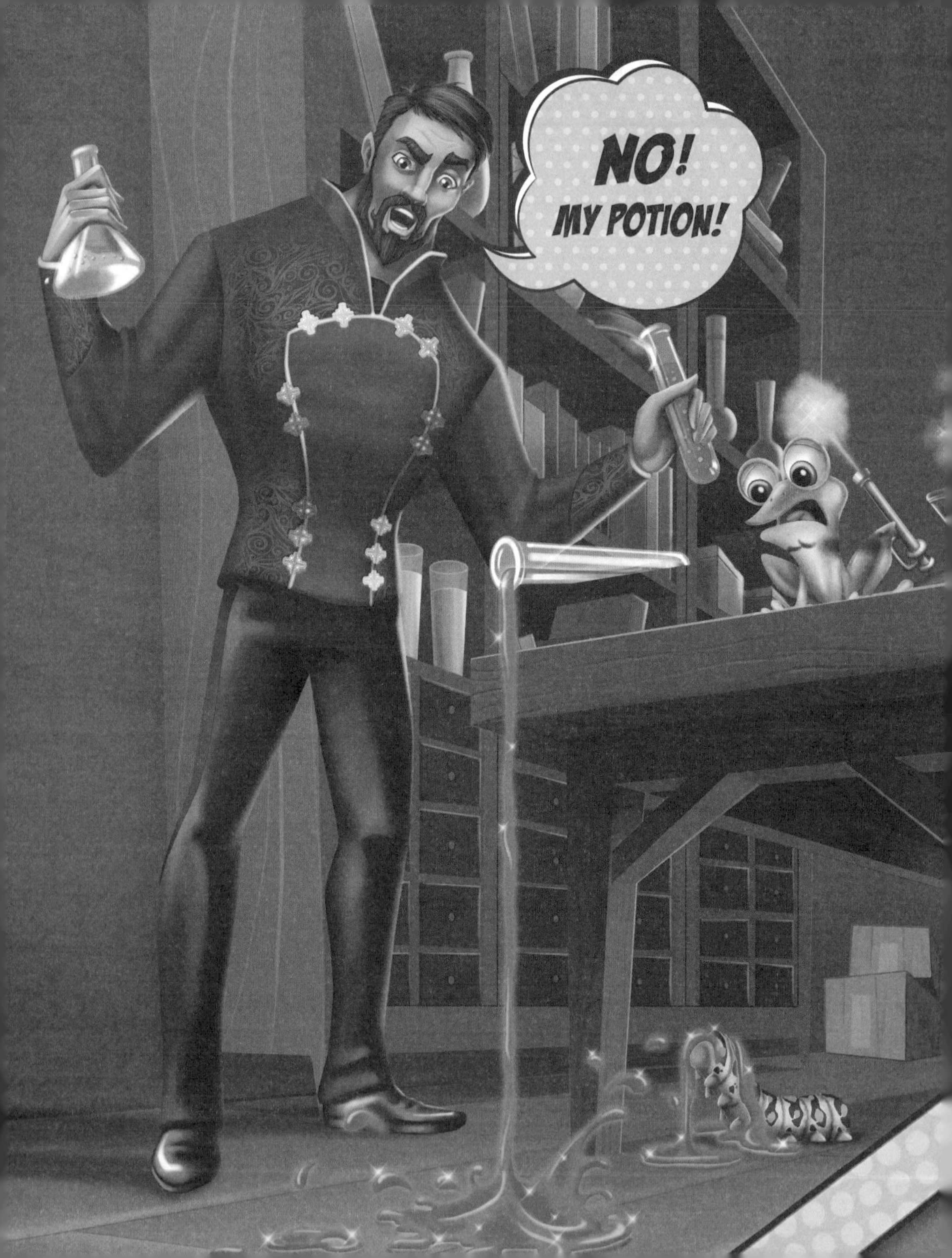
NO!
MY POTION!

Danger was indeed lurking. The royal advisor, a ruthless man named Baron Von Ravendale, had created a potion that would give him superpowers. He plotted to use these powers to take over the kingdom.

Just as the baron was about to drink the potion, his pet frog flicked out his tongue to nab a fly—and knocked the potion over!

The potion spilled out onto a cute little caterpillar. Soon after, the caterpillar transformed into a magical sparkle butterfly!

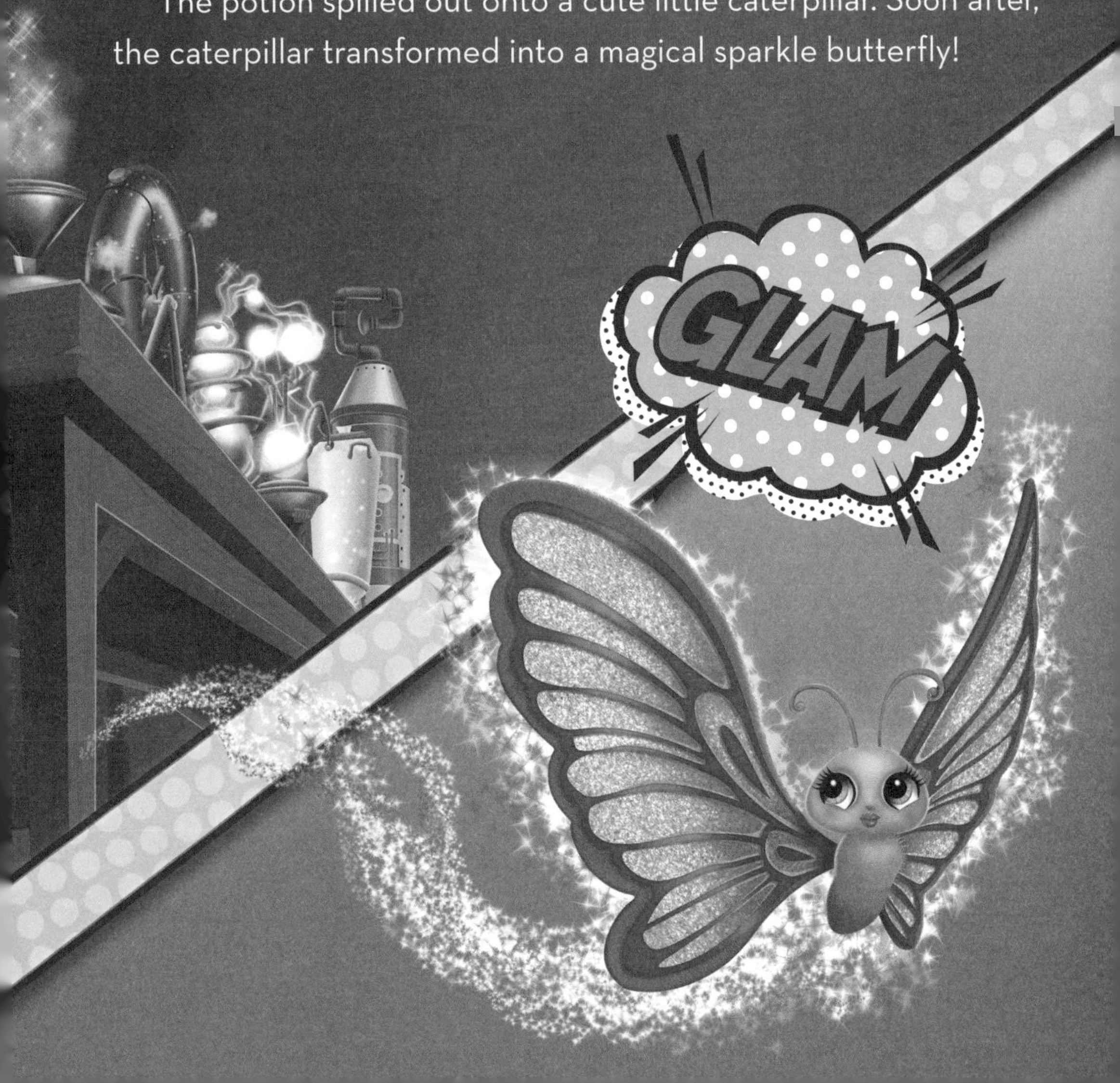
GLAM

The next day, Kara was having tea with her friends and her cousin Corinne when the sparkle butterfly appeared.

"A bug!" cried Corinne, trying to squash it.

"Don't!" cried Kara. She saved the butterfly, and it kissed her. As it fluttered away, Kara felt dizzy. Madison and Makalya helped her to bed.

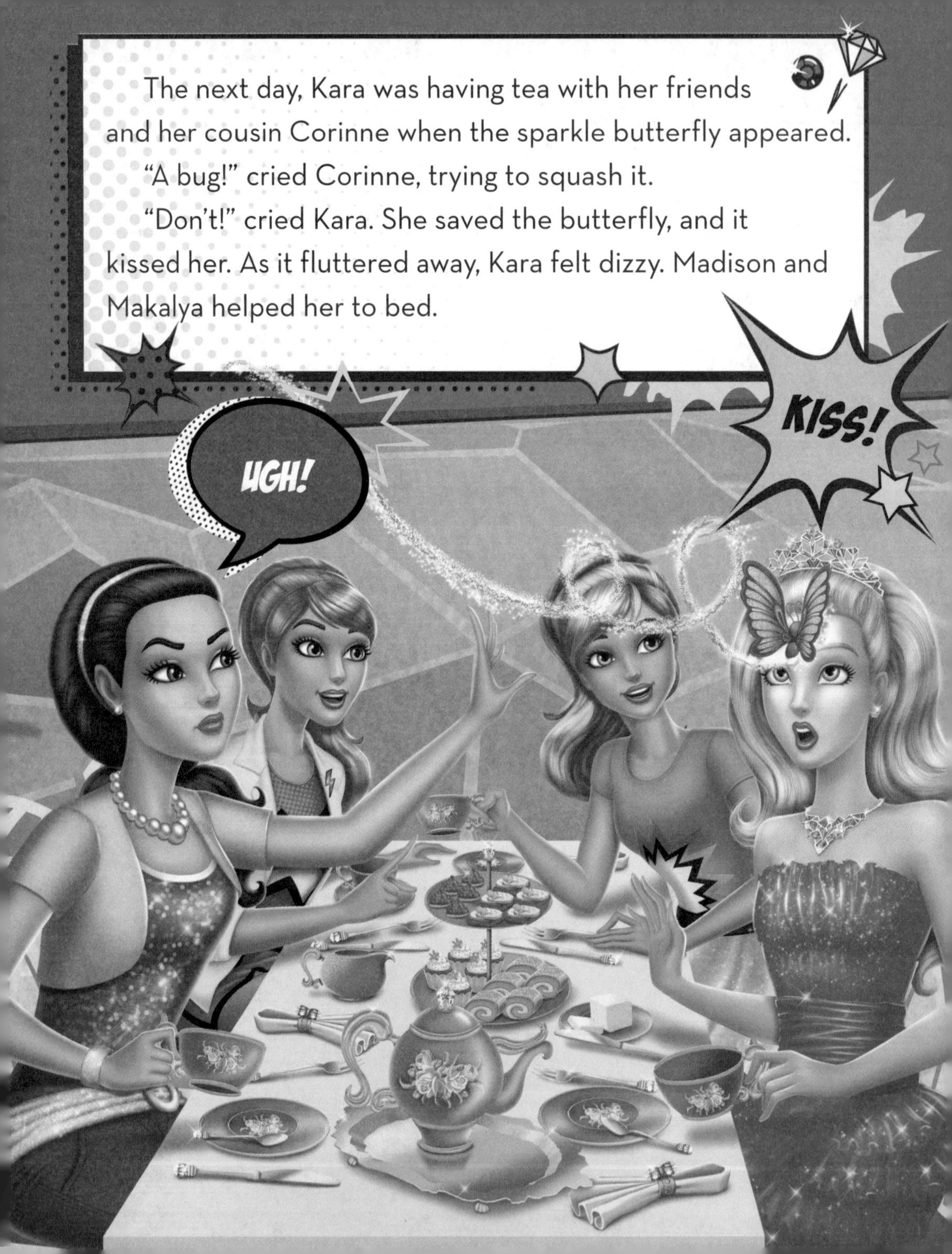
UGH!
KISS!

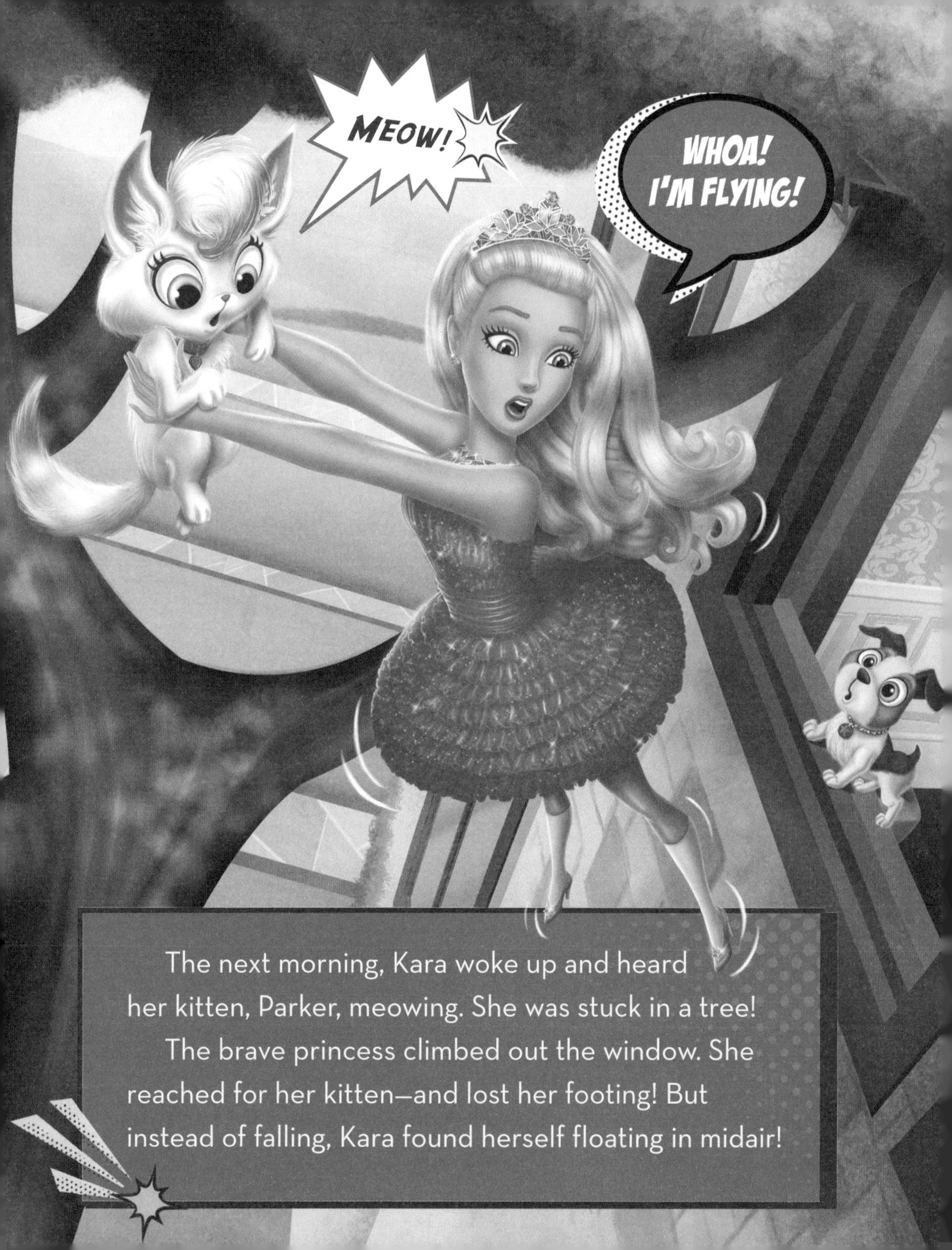
MEOW!
WHOA!
I'M FLYING!

The next morning, Kara woke up and heard her kitten, Parker, meowing. She was stuck in a tree!

The brave princess climbed out the window. She reached for her kitten—and lost her footing! But instead of falling, Kara found herself floating in midair!

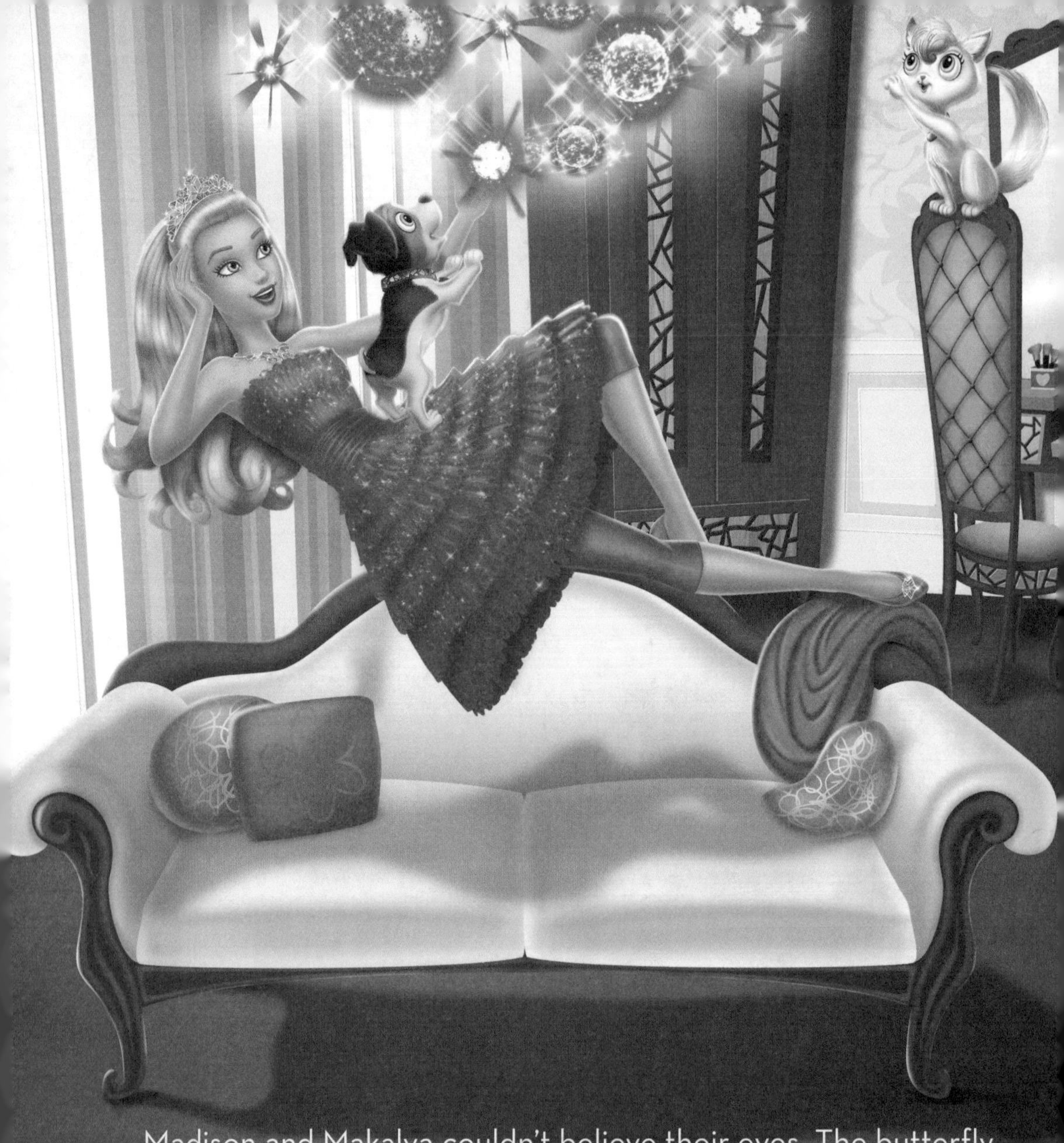

Madison and Makalya couldn't believe their eyes. The butterfly kiss had given Kara superpowers! She could float, she could fly, she had superstrength, and she could shoot pink sparkle orbs!

"You're a superhero!" gasped Madison.

"You've got princess power!" cheered Makalya.

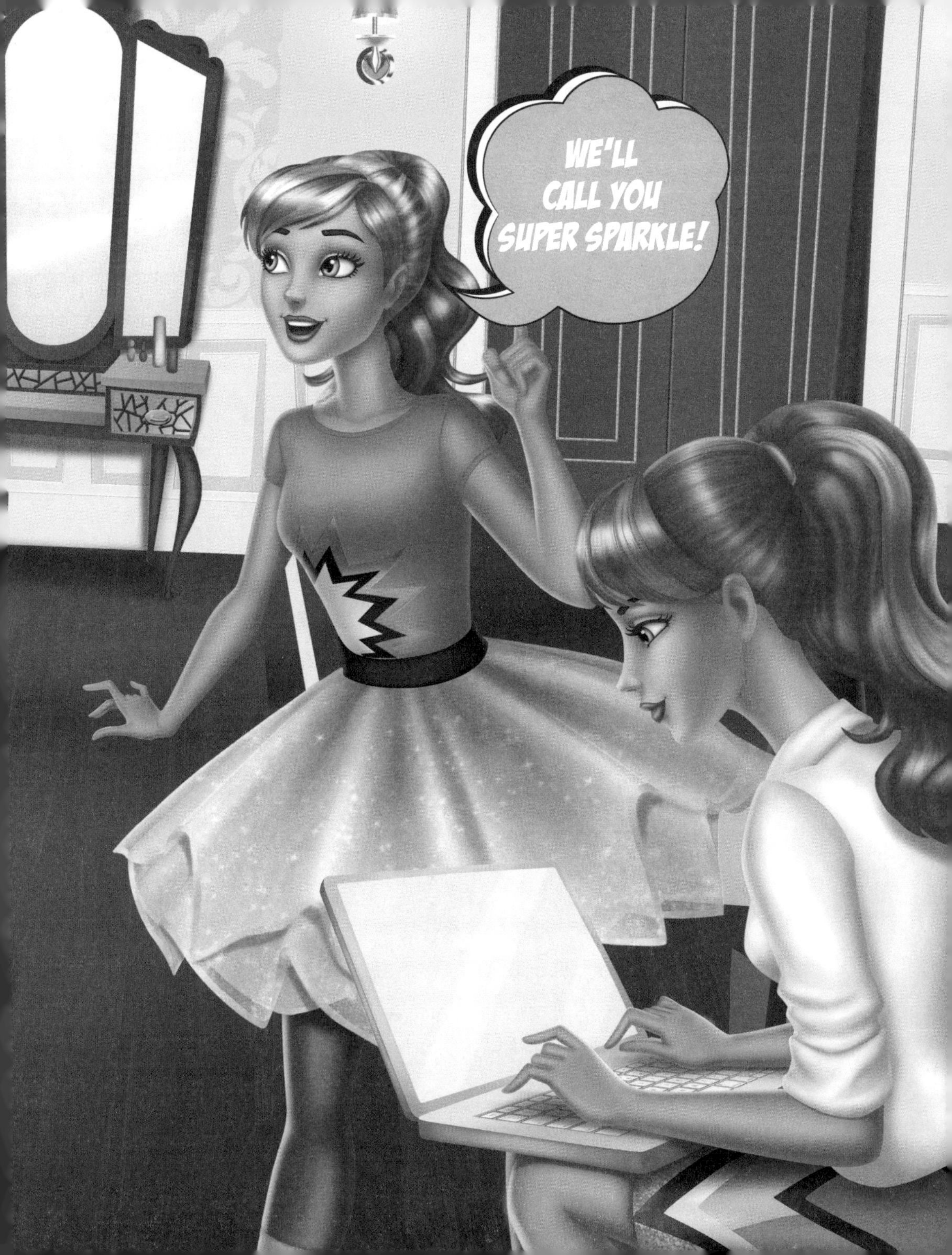
WE'LL
CALL YOU
SUPER SPARKLE!

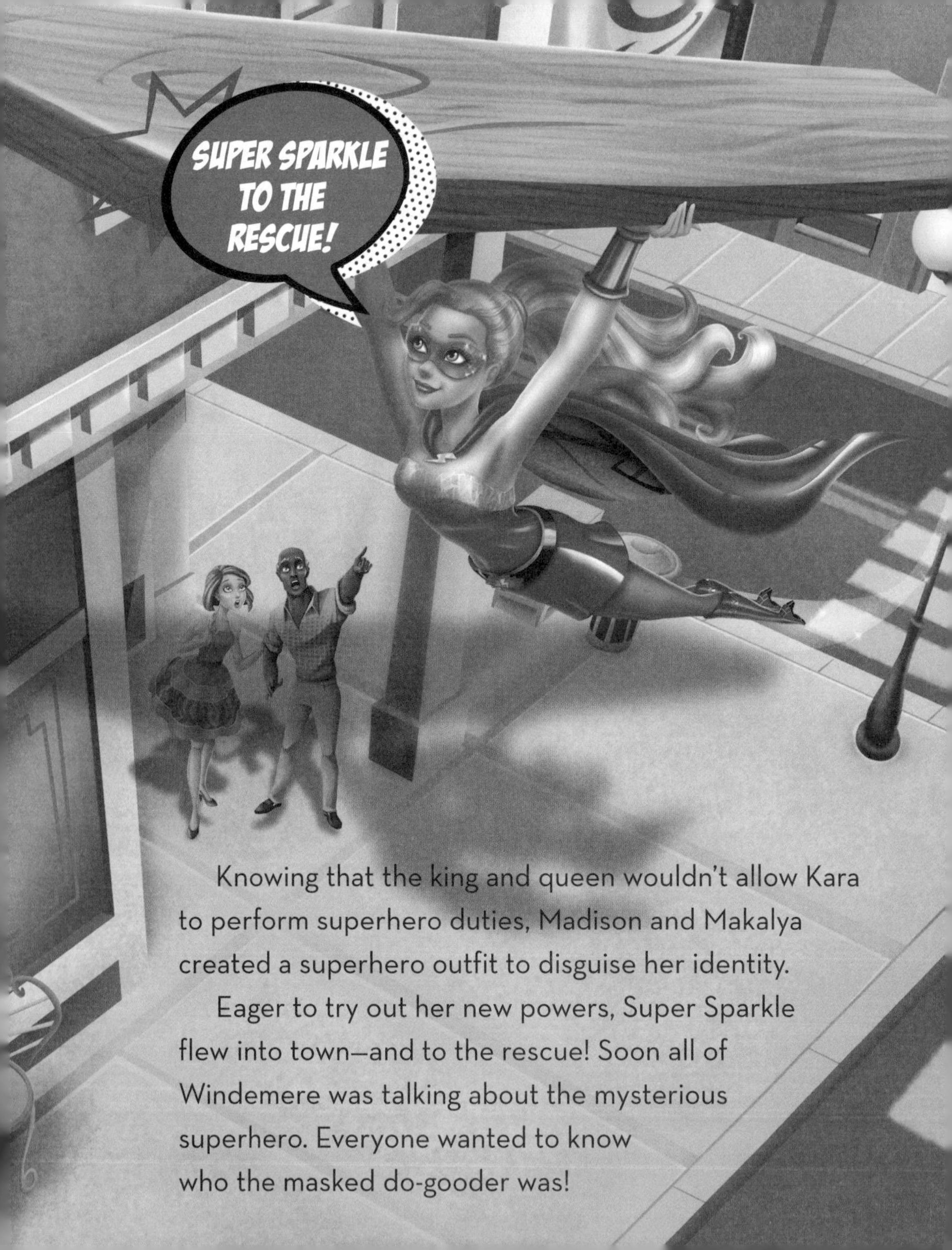
SUPER SPARKLE TO THE RESCUE!

Knowing that the king and queen wouldn't allow Kara to perform superhero duties, Madison and Makalya created a superhero outfit to disguise her identity.

Eager to try out her new powers, Super Sparkle flew into town—and to the rescue! Soon all of Windemere was talking about the mysterious superhero. Everyone wanted to know who the masked do-gooder was!

It wasn't easy for Kara to hide her new identity. One evening as she was changing back into her princess clothes, Corinne secretly spotted her.

Corinne wanted to be a superhero, too. She discovered the secret behind Kara's superpowers, found the sparkle butterfly . . .

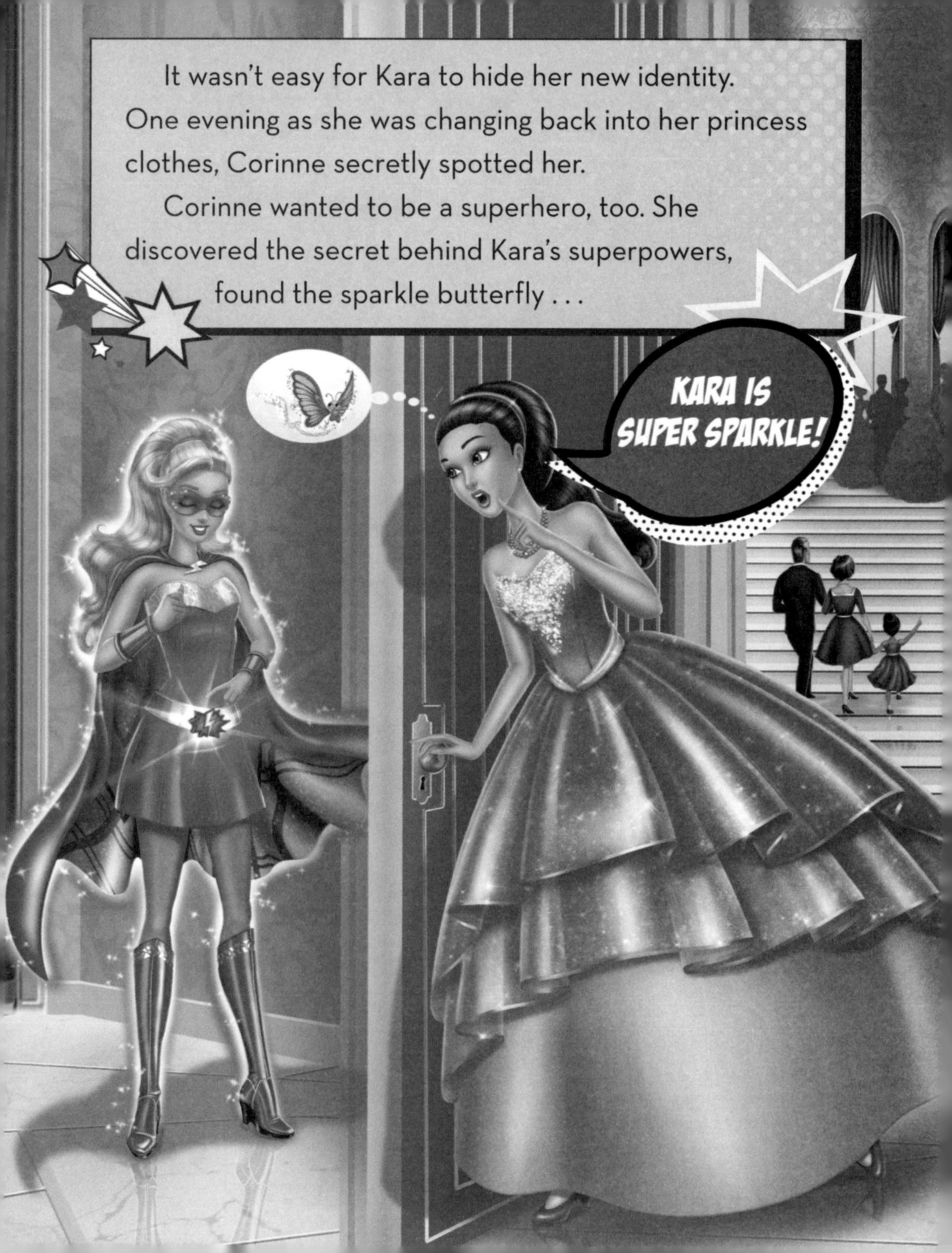
KARA IS SUPER SPARKLE!

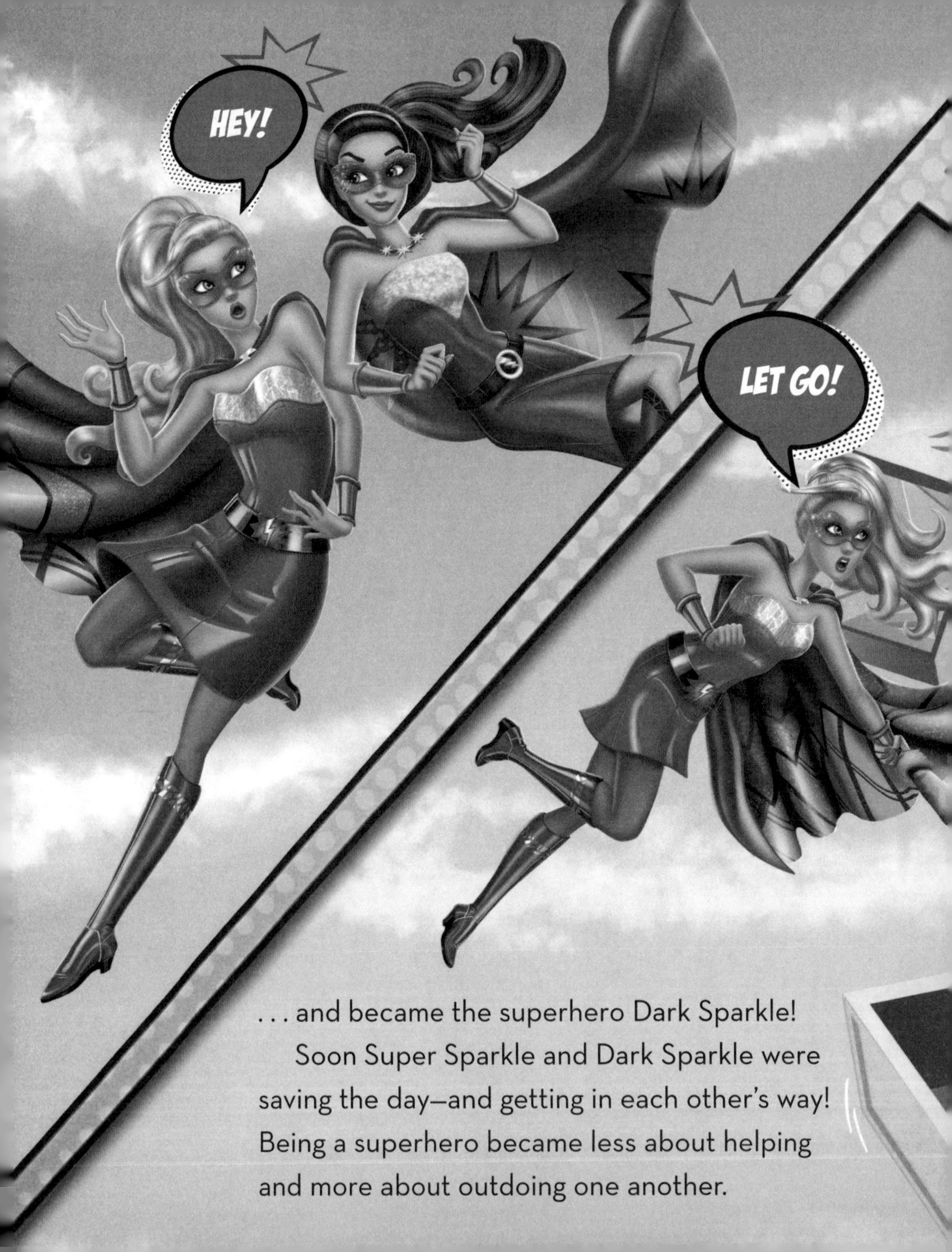
HEY!
LET GO!

. . . and became the superhero Dark Sparkle!

Soon Super Sparkle and Dark Sparkle were saving the day—and getting in each other's way! Being a superhero became less about helping and more about outdoing one another.

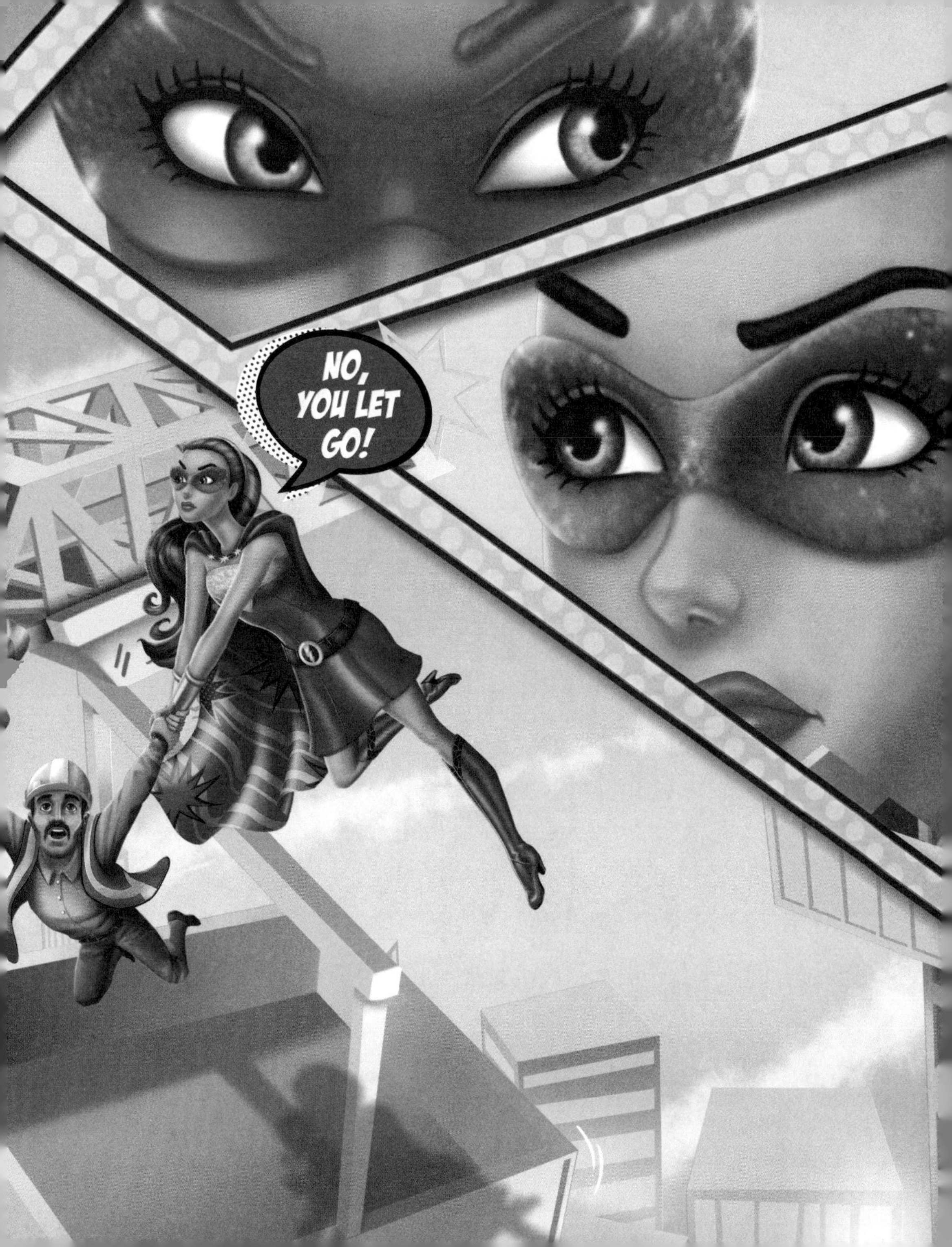
NO, YOU LET GO!

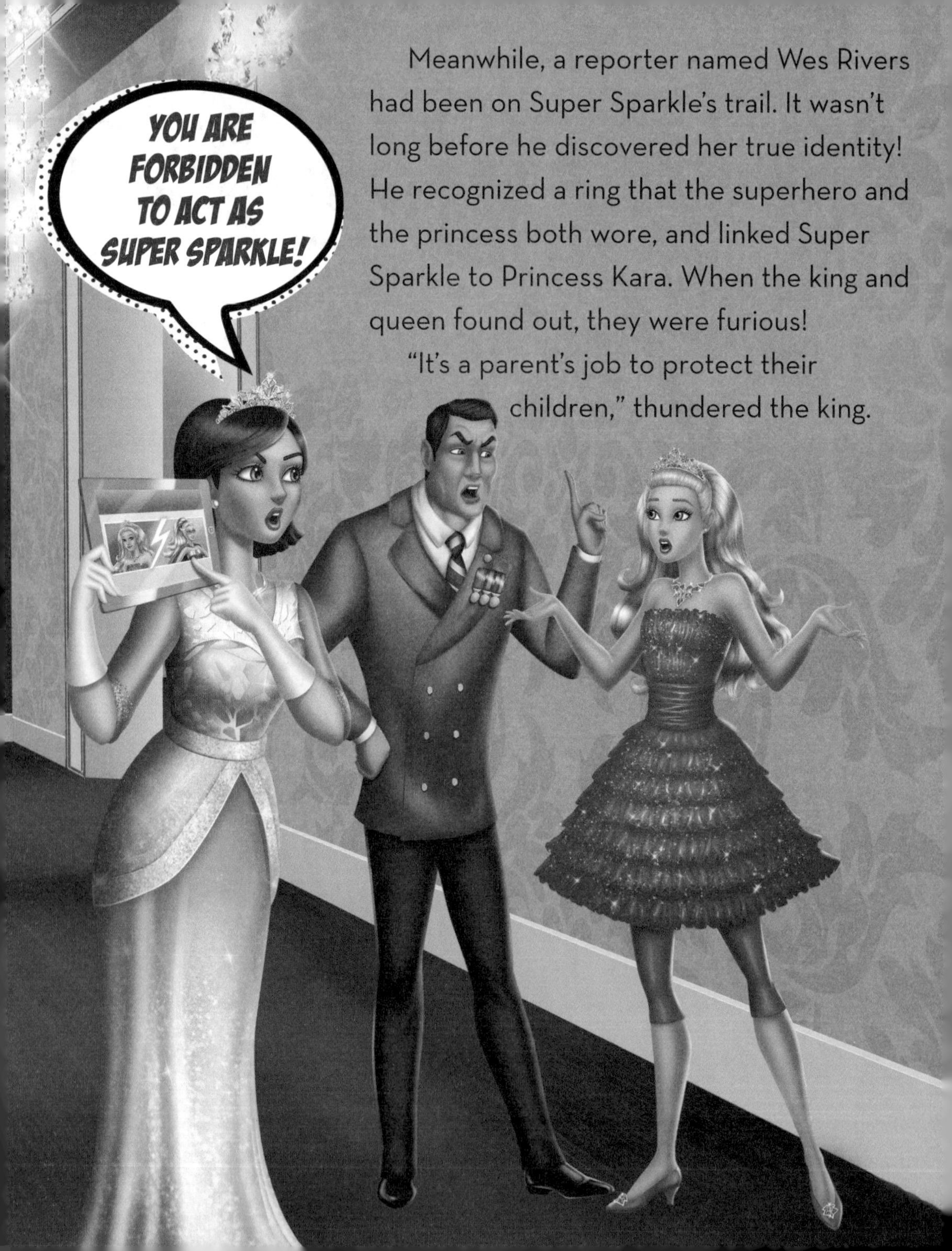
YOU ARE FORBIDDEN TO ACT AS SUPER SPARKLE!

Meanwhile, a reporter named Wes Rivers had been on Super Sparkle's trail. It wasn't long before he discovered her true identity! He recognized a ring that the superhero and the princess both wore, and linked Super Sparkle to Princess Kara. When the king and queen found out, they were furious!

"It's a parent's job to protect their children," thundered the king.

In his secret lab, Baron Von Ravendale reconstructed his magical superhero potion and drank deeply—and so did his frog, Bruce.

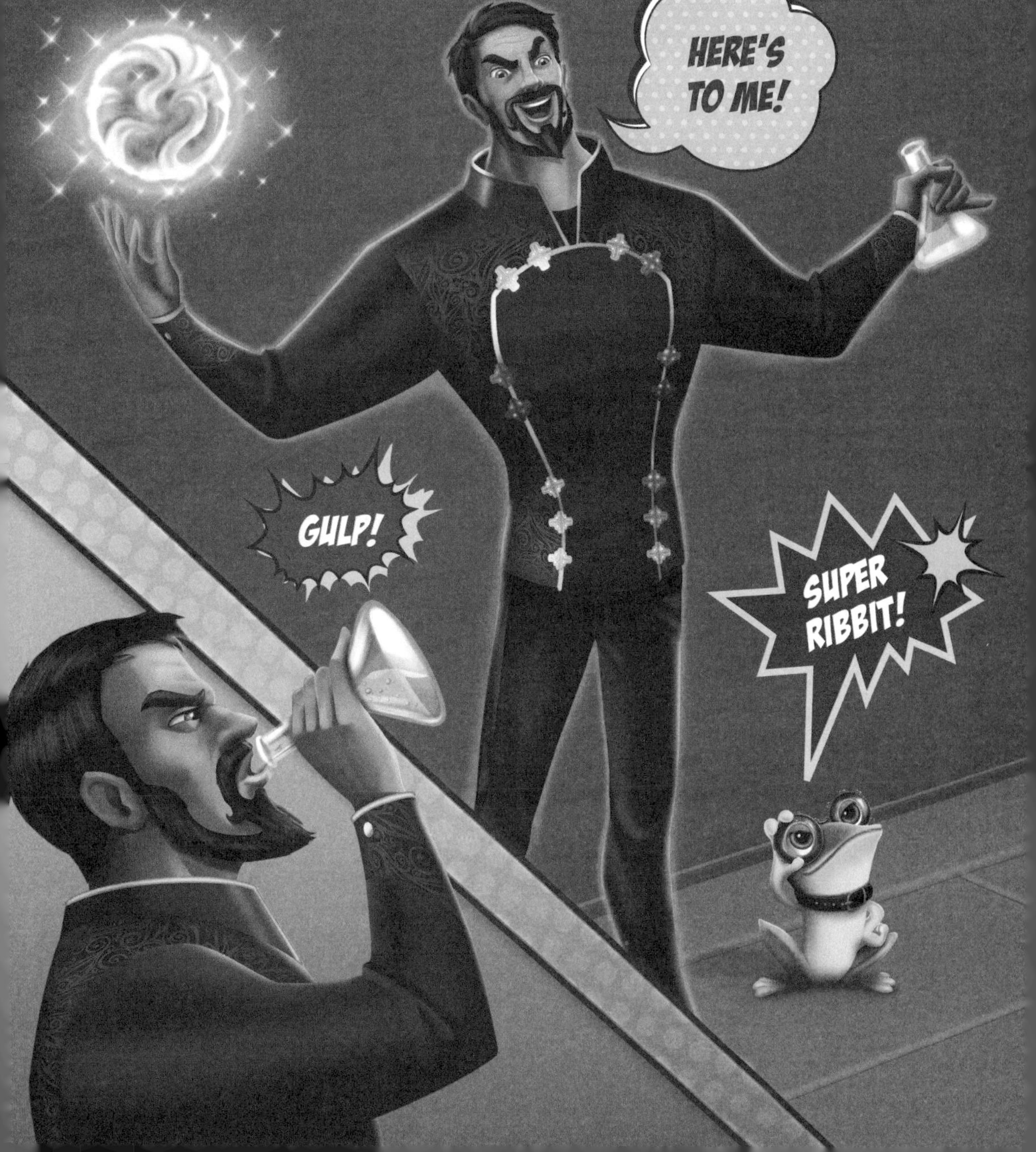
HERE'S TO ME!
GULP!
SUPER RIBBIT!

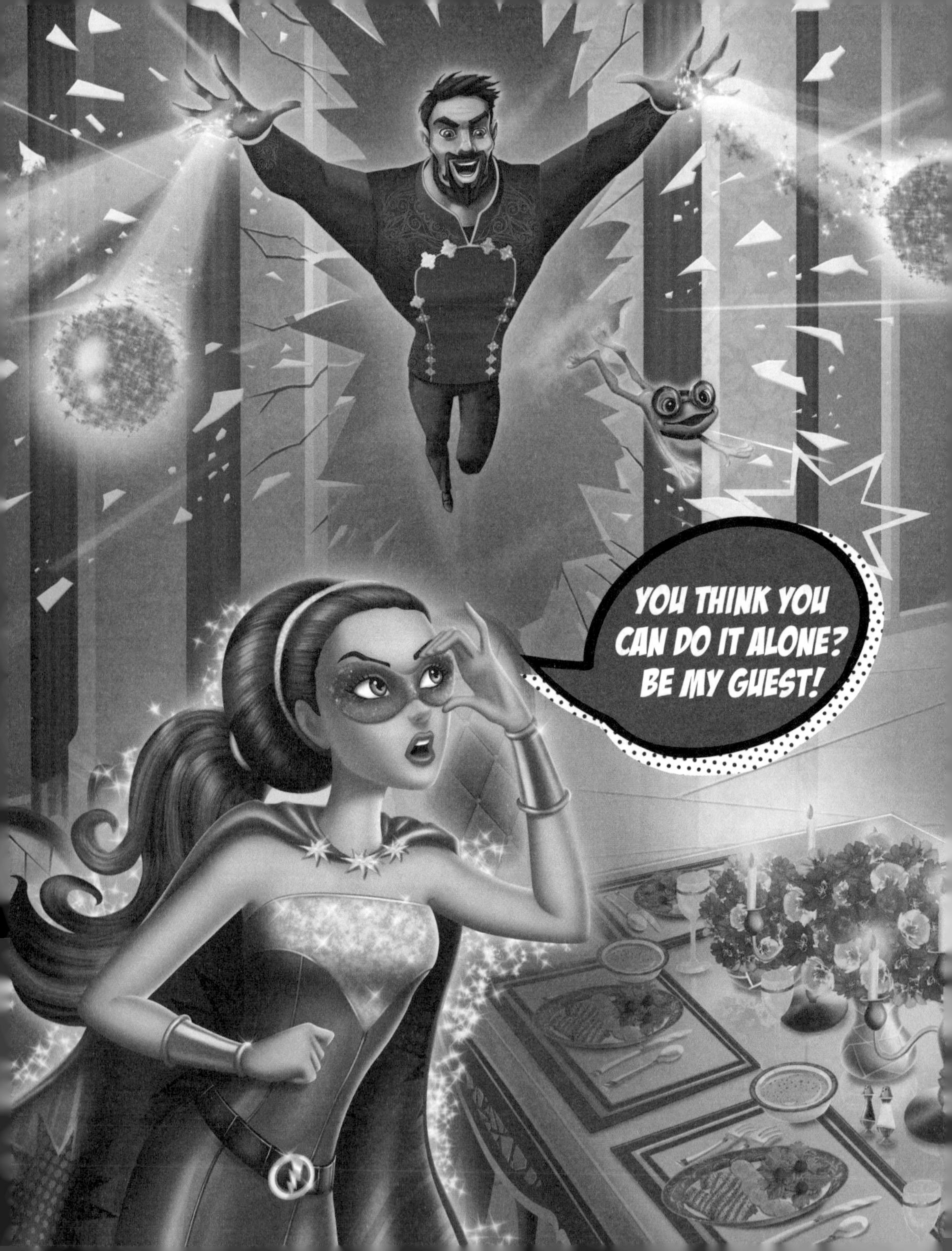
YOU THINK YOU CAN DO IT ALONE? BE MY GUEST!

That night, the baron burst in on the royal family as they were sitting down to dinner. "Windemere is mine!" he shouted, blasting orbs of dark energy at the king and queen.

Kara and Corinne quickly transformed into Super Sparkle and Dark Sparkle.

But Super Sparkle didn't want to share the spotlight.

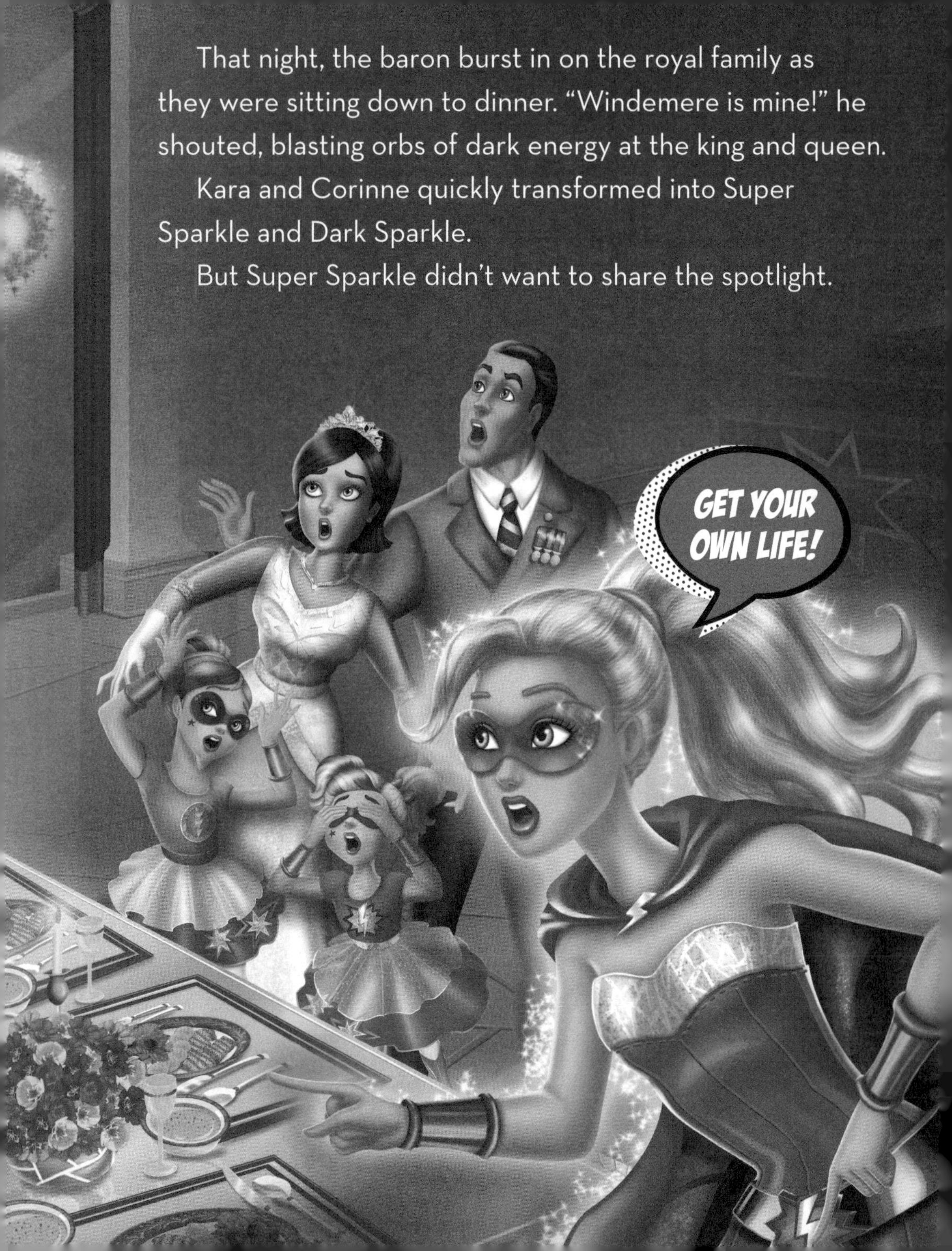
GET YOUR OWN LIFE!

Dark Sparkle flew off, and Super Sparkle battled the baron alone. "There's more than one way to destroy a king!" cried the baron. He blasted a dormant volcano and lava erupted out of it, heading straight for the castle!

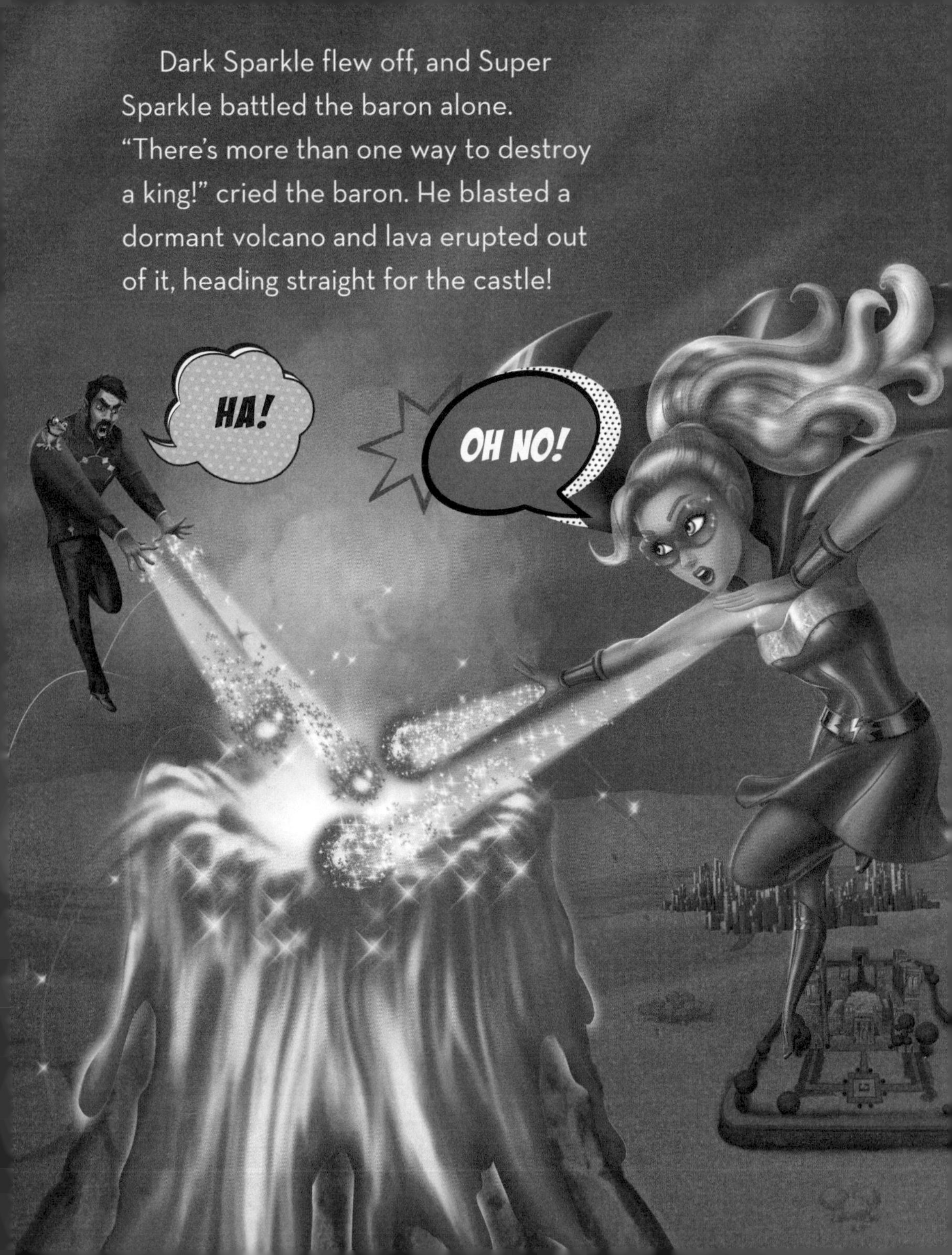
HA!
OH NO!

Super Sparkle tried to stop the lava, but it was flowing too fast.

Suddenly, Dark Sparkle joined her.

"Corinne!" exclaimed Super Sparkle.

"You'd never walk away from this, and neither can I," said Dark Sparkle.

"If we can divert the flow away from the castle and toward the lake . . . ," began Super Sparkle.

"Maybe we can cool things off!" finished Dark Sparkle.

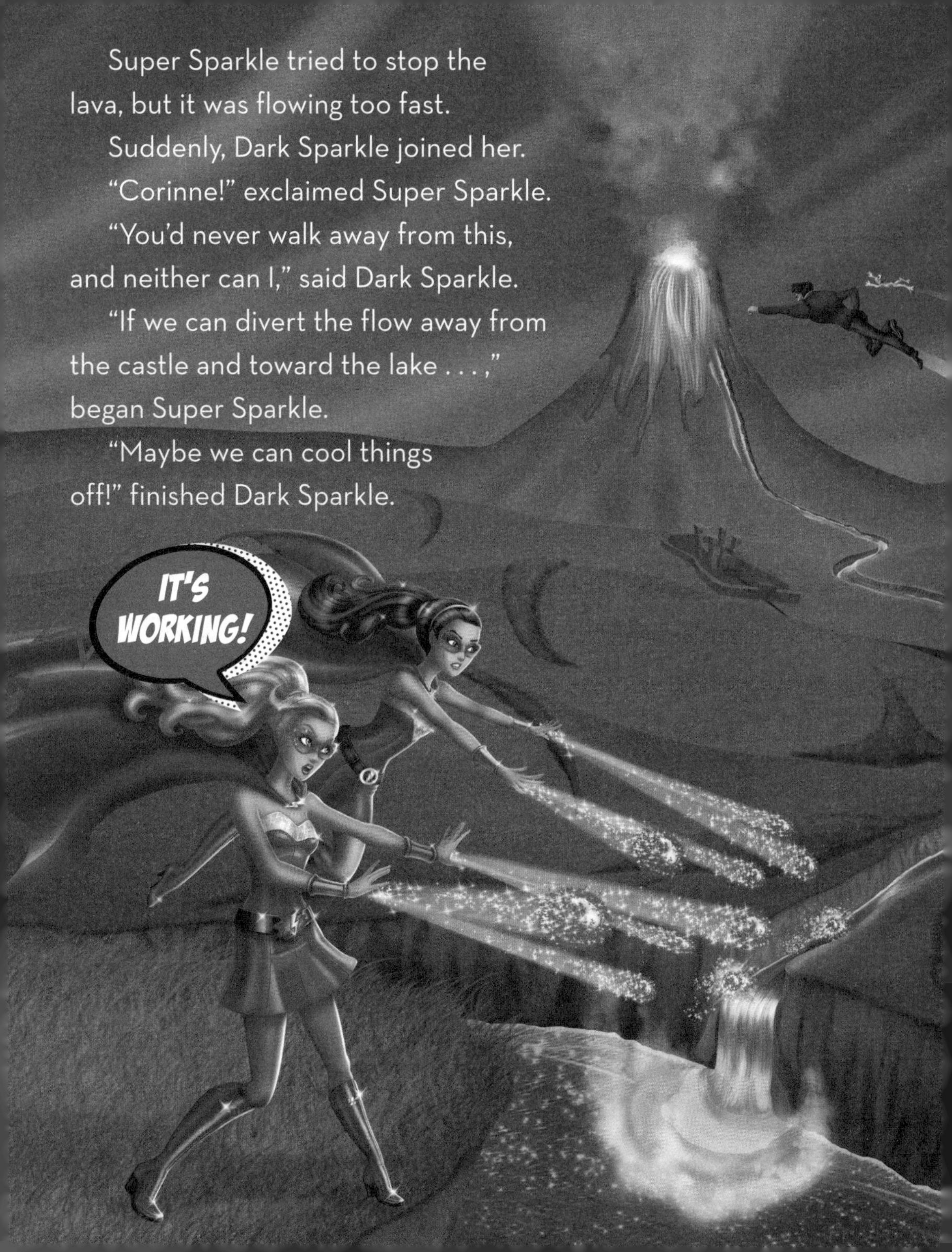
IT'S WORKING!

Working together, Super Sparkle and Dark Sparkle saved the castle from the volcano—but they still had to defeat Baron Von Ravendale!

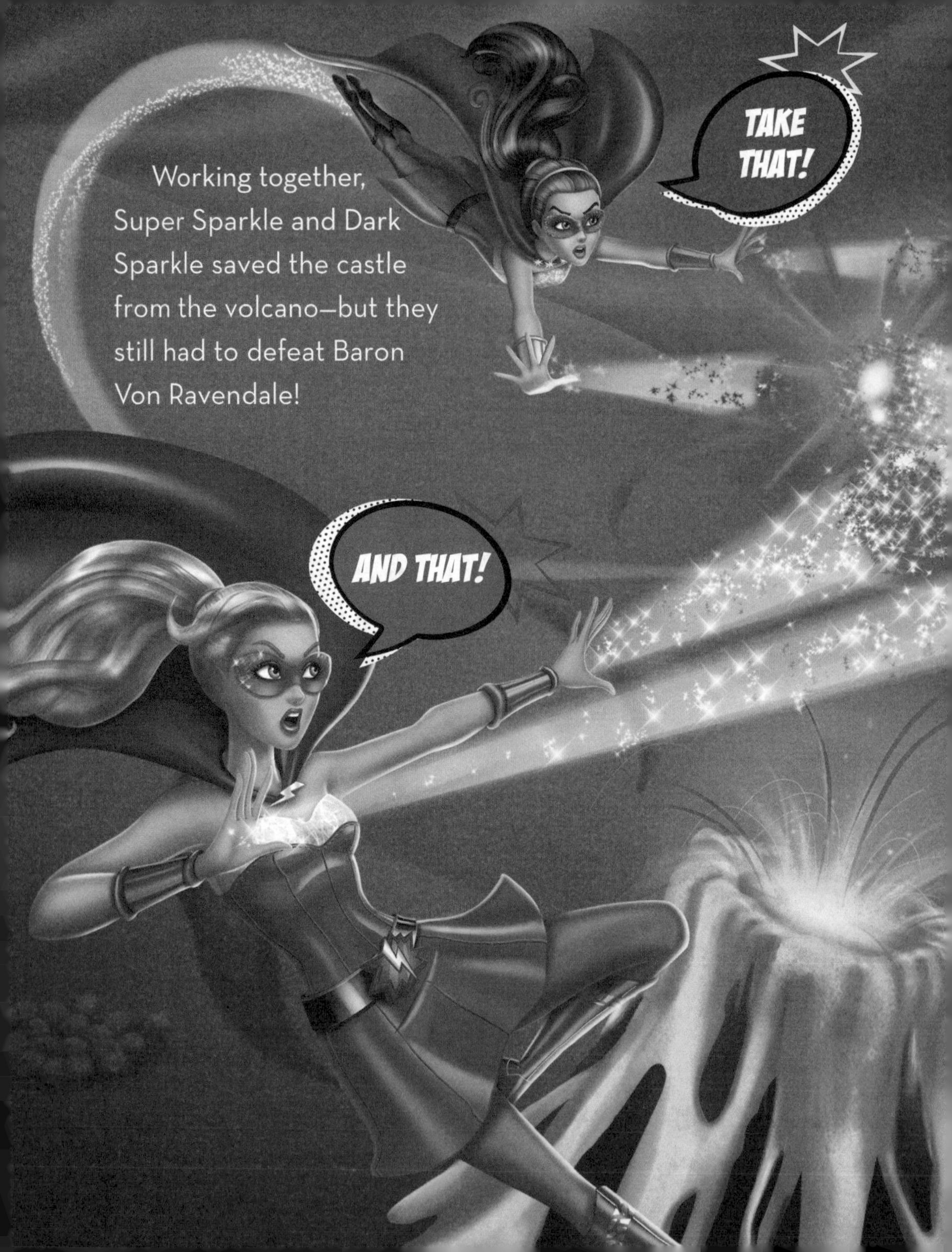
TAKE THAT!
AND THAT!

"You think this is over, Twinkle Twins?" the baron called, shooting dark magic orbs at them.

"*Twinkle Twins?*" gasped Super Sparkle.

"You are so going down," declared Dark Sparkle.

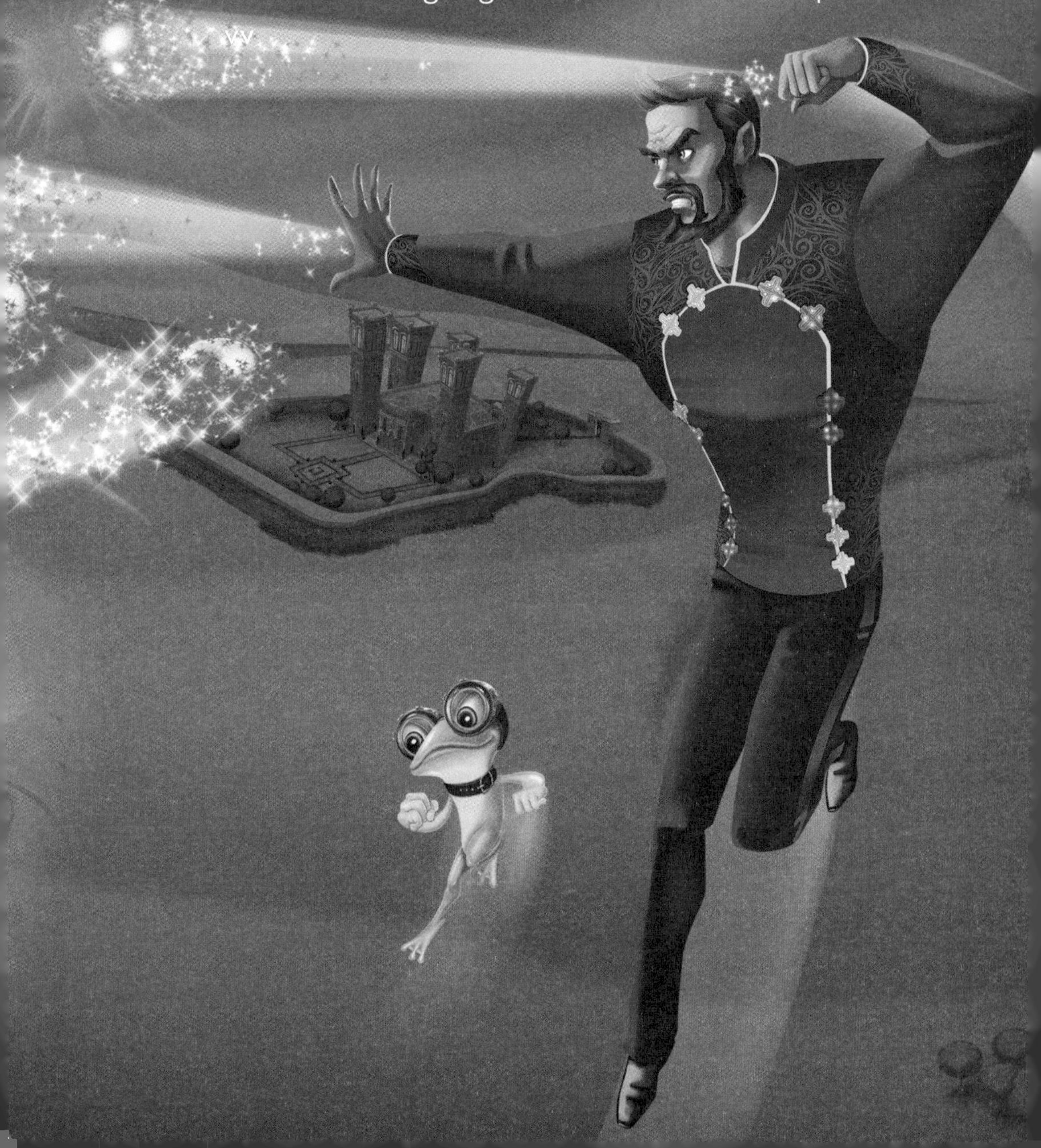

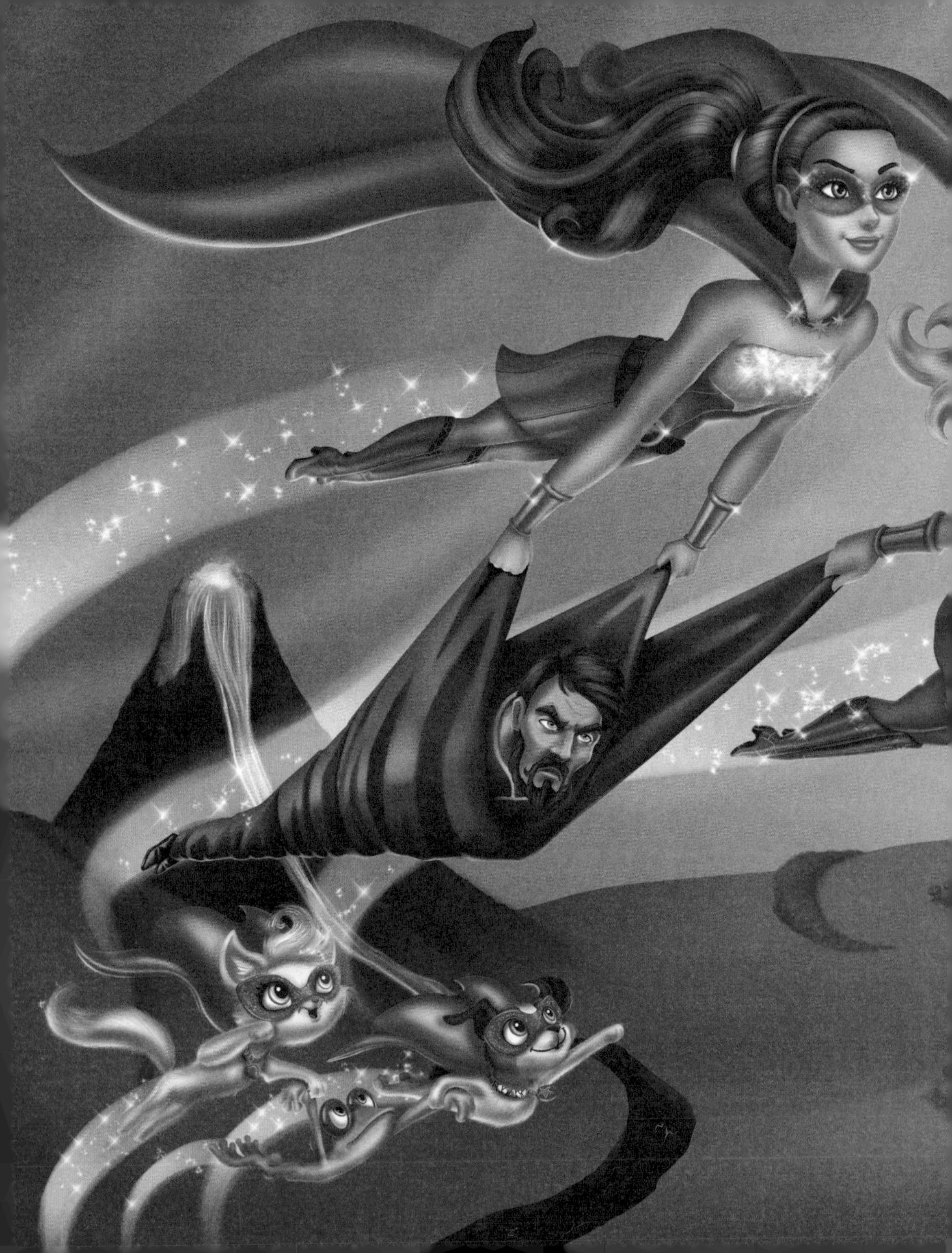

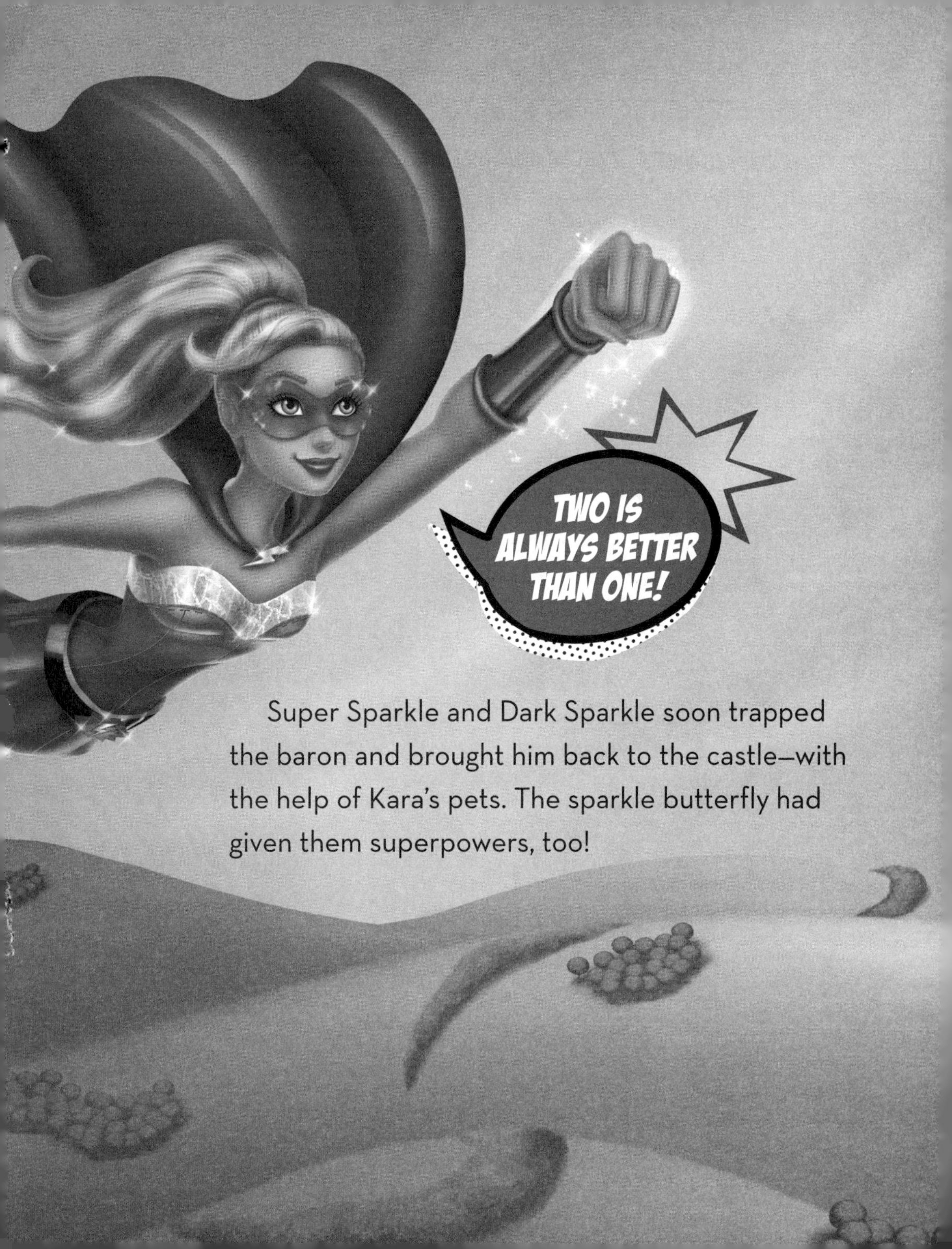
TWO IS ALWAYS BETTER THAN ONE!

Super Sparkle and Dark Sparkle soon trapped the baron and brought him back to the castle—with the help of Kara's pets. The sparkle butterfly had given them superpowers, too!

The king and queen thanked Kara and Corinne.

"You not only proved to be able to take care of yourselves, you took care of *us*, too. We're proud of you both," said the king.

Kara smiled. "And now the kingdom's got *two* superheroes watching its back!"

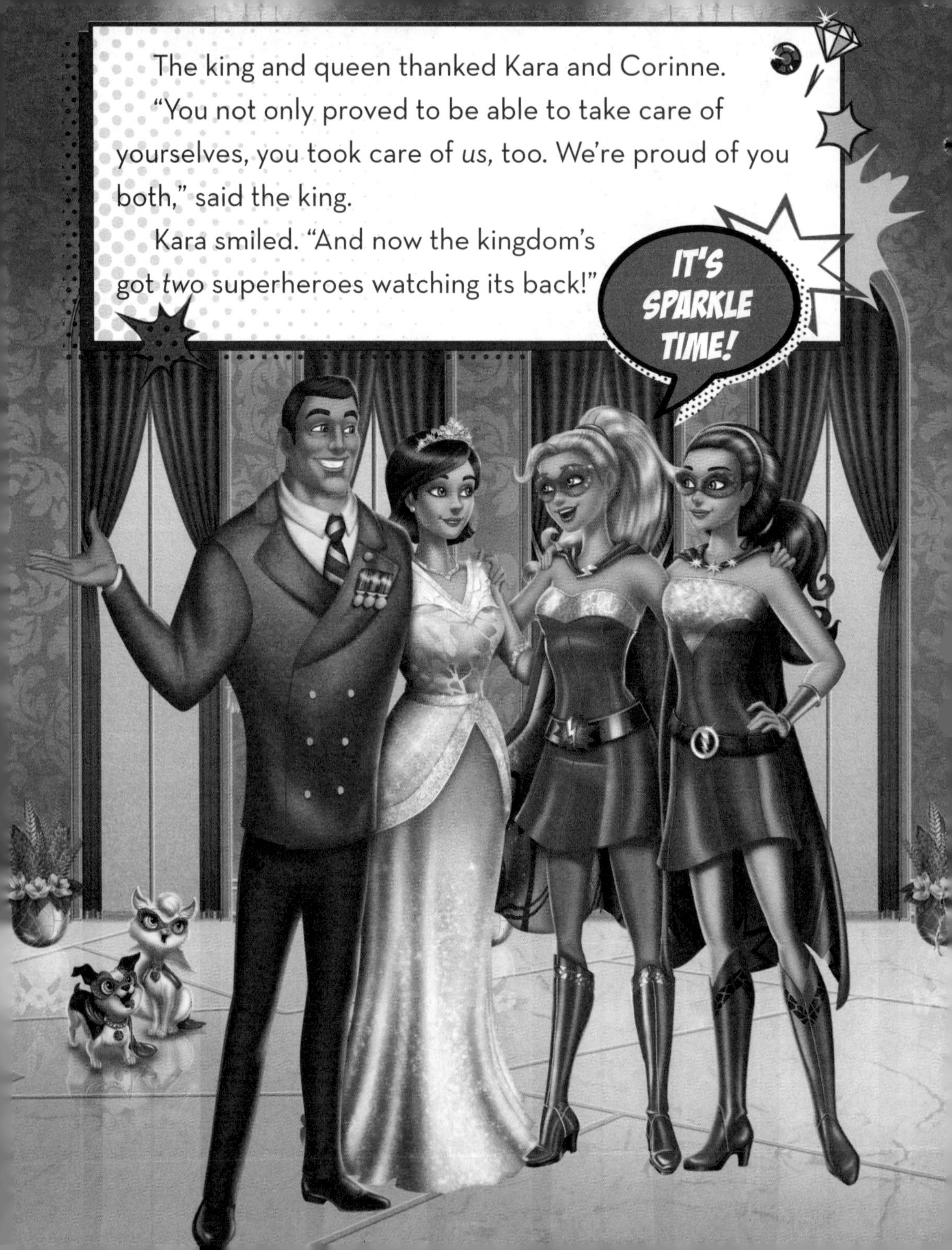
IT'S SPARKLE TIME!